For Imogen & Phoebe, with love
R.H.

For Smriti, who asked me to do the book
B.C.

Art created with watercolor
Typeset in Aunt Mildred
Book design by Ian Butterworth

First published in Great Britain by Bloomsbury Publishing Plc.
Published in the United States by Bloomsbury U.S.A. Children's Books
175 Fifth Avenue, New York, New York 10010

Library of Congress Cataloging-in-Publication Data
Hamilton, Richard.
If I were you / by Richard Hamilton ; illustrated by Babette Cole. — 1st U.S. ed.
p.   cm.
Summary: At bedtime, a little girl and her father play a game in which each
imagines what it would be like to be the other for a day.
ISBN-13: 978-1-59990-289-0 • ISBN-10: 1-59990-289-3
[1. Fathers and daughters—Fiction. 2. Imagination—Fiction. 3. Bedtime—Fiction.]
I. Cole, Babette, ill. II. Title.
PZ7.H182658If 2008   [E]—dc22   2008005888

First U.S. Edition 2008
Printed in China
2 4 6 8 10 9 7 5 3 1

If I Were You

Richard Hamilton

illustrated by

Babette Cole

BLOOMSBURY
CHILDREN'S
BOOKS

Dad tucked Daisy into bed.

He said, "If I were you, I'd snuggle down and go to sleep."

"But you're not me," said Daisy.

"I know . . . but if I were." Dad yawned.

And that got Daisy thinking . . .

"If you were me and I were you," Daisy said,
"I'd read you a story about three bears.

Then I'd say good night
and go downstairs!"

"If you were me and I were you," said Dad,
"I'd go to sleep with Kangaroo,

and in the morning, we'd bounce on you!"

"If you were me and I were you," said Daisy,
"I'd dress you in a **pink tutu!**

I'd give you **oatmeal** every day

Dad sat up and stroked his chin.
"If you were me—now let me see—
while you washed up, I'd watch TV!

Then I could play with Millie mouse,
while you made beds and tidied the house!"

Daisy wasn't sure about **that!**
She said, "Then we'd go out for a walk.
I'd push your stroller round the block."

"What?" said Dad.
"Past the neighbors? Dressed in pink?
Can you imagine what they'd think?"

"If I were you and you were me," said Daisy,
"I'd take you to the zoo to see
the baby elephants and cheetahs,
the crocodiles and anteaters!"

Dad clapped his hands and said,
"Could we take the bus and buy balloons?
Eat ice cream and see baboons?"

"Yes, if you were very, **very** good," said Daisy,
"and behaved **exactly** as you should."

"And after the zoo, could we play in the park and stay out till it's really dark?"
Daisy folded her arms.

"We could go to the park but not for long.
You're so heavy and I'm not that strong."

"After the park we'd have cake and tea
with your friends and Mommy and Baby and me.

And you could play games like musical chairs
and hot potato and tag with the bears."

"And then a bath to make me clean,
with ducks and bubbles and submarines?"

"I'd make you wash your face and hair, behind your ears ... everywhere!"

"And then I'd tuck you into bed
and give you a big kiss on your head."
    Dad sighed. "What a day! I'd think I was dreaming—
no washing, no cooking, no driving, no cleaning!
Wouldn't it be great?"

Daisy looked at her dad.

She said, "Dad, if I were you and you were me ...

...I think I'd rather still be me!"

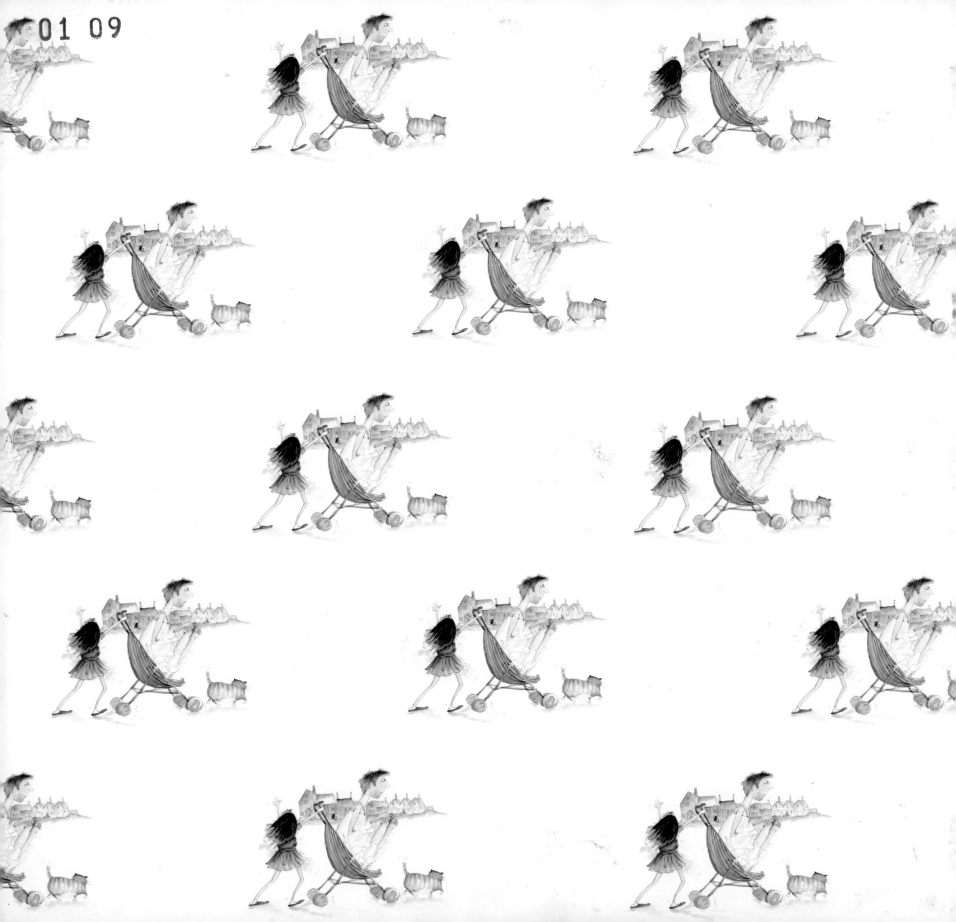